What life teaches you

firdos tarannum

pencil

ISBN 978-93-5667-020-4
© firdos tarannum 2022
Published in India 2022 by Pencil

A brand of
One Point Six Technologies Pvt. Ltd.
123, Building J2, Shram Seva Premises,
Wadala Truck Terminal, Wadala (E)
Mumbai 400037, Maharashtra, INDIA
E connect@thepencilapp.com
W www.thepencilapp.com

Author biography

Firdos Tarannum is a teacher , with a degree in bachelor of science.
She completed her school education in holy family school of Sindhanur, and completed her science field education in a renowned college called smj pu college, sindhanur.

Firdos Tarannum always admired of educating herself and others around her , she lived her life to the fullest before marriage and Alhamdulillah her every dream of educating the children completed.
She taught some religious topics to the students of an islamic school where her parents studied which was a stepping stone of her teaching field, she completed the degree and started teaching in the same year immersing herself into two different roles everyday.
She also gave tuition classes for the kids and also actively participated in courses of Islamic organisation held every week and ten days in summer months
She also served as a science teacher in her own learned school for a year , which was a proud moment for her teacher seeing their student sitting with them on the same post at such an early stage.
Lockdown throughout the world stopped the teaching of many teachers and one among them was firdos too.

She completed her degree on the other hand successfully just before lockdown.

During the times of lockdown she used them in a good way by handling around motivational or councilling sessions as her second dream is to help people with her words which have an immense effect on one's mind as people are often get themselves in depression and stress.

She got married and gave birth to a wonderful son in a year of marriage itself Alhamdulillah. But this didn't stop her from completing her dreams.

Tarannum is a housewife and a mother, who recently inspired herself to write the books after finding her love towards studies, she loved reading and was always appreciated for her work either for her teaching of 3 years or a councilling sessions.With her support of her spouse she now balances her work,child and book

Her only dream is to, then to try have a weekend class for neighborhood children and often conduct workshop for dealing with mental health. At the same time , keeping herself educated and learn something everyday and teach something often so that this journey of her is continued by her children in sha Allah.

If one loves something truly then it is the sole responsibility of oneself to take care of surroundings and their talent as well while fulfilling all their responsibilities

CONTENTS

Epigraph

In the name of Allah, the Entirely Merciful, the Especially Merciful.

[All] praise is [due] to Allah, Lord of the worlds – The Entirely Merciful, the Especially Merciful,

Sovereign of the Day of Recompense. It is You we worship and You we ask for help.

Guide us to the straight path –The path of those upon whom You have bestowed favor, not of those who have evoked [Your] anger or of those who are astray.

-AAMEEN

Introduction

This book is a collection of small stories from the life of the author , which is very common in every day's life but we fail to realise that life is meant to teach us something everyday-

The small details of every situation can be used to learn something from life which teaches us everyday but we start to feel depressed when calamities reach us and thereby we fail to look at the problems deeply - The problem remains same till you learn or gain something without complaining - life is a journey of learning from birth to the death - The author has tried her best to put her stories in an easy form with a separate section of lessons she has learnt from every story-

The main aim is to let the reader realise and deeply connect it to their live so that they can also learn something .

MEET! AS IT IS LAST

I attended an islamic gathering for a few weeks and one week I had a lecture , after the lecture I met everyone before leaving. one among them was the old woman who said to me "YOUR UPBRINGING IS GOOD". This was the most beautiful line I ever heard from unknown ones after marriage . After few months, she passed away and I couldn't meet her because of lockdown . Many of them said negative things about her but my thinking towards her remained positive because of a single line she said among those weeks and I prayed for her.

<u>LESSON-</u>

- Be kind and talk good who knows your last meeting.

- Meet as if it is your last.

- Do not speak bad about dead one.

- Your words matter mostly after death.

- People praying for you depends on how you behaved with them earlier.

COMPARING LESSENS HAPPINESS

Whenever we had a family gatherings, I usually met a woman who was quite expressive but failed to maintain privacy of her own life. She openly used to express that one or other belongings was gifted by her husband. She overly boasted her husband every time we met, I first thought not to let her thoughts in but after few meetings with her, my behaviour towards my husband changed because of comparision. but later I apologized to my husband and he made me understand that, though you can't change someones behaviour all you have to be is cautious and maintain distance without effecting your relation.

LESSONS-

- Over expressing sometimes may result in evil eye.

- Never boast about your private matter.

- Know what to say and how much.

- Be thankful for what you have instead of comparing.

- Comparision is a rotten seed, which gives rotten fruits or damages the plant.

LEARN FROM EVERTHING

I admire my older sister, but at a certain age, I was jealous as I thought all my family loved only her. After few years, I started to love her as she is my special one because I used to follow whatever she said and more than that I can say my interest towards the religion was because of her. she was the biggest source and blessing in strenghthning my eeman level. I saw her crying while making supplications, I saw her praying tahajjud, crying in sujuud, wearing hijaab,reading and collecting authentic books ,learning arabic, writing and painting islamic quotes ,I loved to see whatever she did for religion and my love towards religion grew as I saw her growing up in religion.

LESSON-

- See positive in others and you will benefit yourself first.

- The More you concentrate on negative side, more will be your sadness and lesser will be your emaan.

- Learn from everyone and love everyone.

- Actions speak louder than the words.

- Be a source of guidance for others.

STAND FOR RIGHT

During our school time, After the christmas function, we went back to class for attendance. when all of a sudden one of our classmates entered by smashing the benches, which made our manager angry and thus, he entered in anger and punched on the face of a boy, whom he thought had done this. All of us were silent watching this, before he could proceed to beat him again. I stood up straight saying "sir, he isn't the one who did this" and there by revealed the real name. everybody stood stunned at my Courageous behaviour. yet, the boy who was innocent was already extremely hurt because of the beating.

<u>Lessons -</u>

- Be just no matter what.

- Do not fear to stand for the right thing.

- If you prefer to be silent by watching the unjust behaviour, it will haunt you and make you regret.

- Regret will haunt you if you remain silent .

- There is no humanity in a human if he stands silent/idle by watching the violence.

SILENCE IS THE BEST ANSWER

I was in class 7, when an incident left the class in shock. Our school's Assistant manager was taking the class. I was the class leader, and he asked me to stand up and i did so. He asked me "do you give notes on the board on your own and not your teachers do this?". i said "yes!. upon the completion of a certain chapter, i give notes as the teacher orders" . To this, he responded with a tight slap on my face. I didn't made an issue but cried hardly over it. But this didn't go well with my teachers, and thus they reacted which made the assistant manager to feel guilty and he later apologized for it.

Lessons -

- It is not good to react to everything.

- silence is the best response.

- you will never regret being silent.

- silence is a weapon which affects hard without any loss.

- Silence doesn't mean compromising with your self-respect.

- Silence makes you strong but takes more time.

- silence needs more strength than speaking.

IT IS OK TO CRY

My infant was shifted to the NICU. I went to see him a day later after giving him birth, but i was not allowed to touch him. on the 5th day, I was allowed to feed him and i waited for 4 hours but was sent back as my baby couldn't cope . Two days later on the day of eid (ramadan) i took him in my arms to feed for the very first time. The tears were flowing all the time. I managed to hold them in the hospital but when my husband hugged me i was broke I kept Saying "what have they done to my child, he is all covered with needles he has become Lean', That was the first time when i felt the feeling of being a mother. And finally after ten days, i brought him back but, this incident still fills my eyes with tears.

<u>Lessons -</u>

- Sometimes it is fine to cry out and let the pain go away.

- crying is not a sign of a weak person.

- crying near Allah, gives you strength and refreshes your heart.

- Holding your pain doesn't make you strong, it just makes one numb and insensitive.

- Remember, Everything has an end

TRY AND LEAVE UPON ALLAH

I was in the labour room, when hours of contraction were in the end phase and i was about to deliver, all of my energy was lost as i had nothing in my stomach and nor i could bear the pain. But, at last i gave birth to a baby boy but due to my low-energy level, He couldn't cry. With very little opened eyes, i could see doctors rushing and trying hard to make him cry by patting, But everything went in vain. I only remembered The last line i said before fainting was " o Allah, it was my duty to carry him for these months, and deliver him by enduring the pain, it's up to you now, for verily you are the one who gives and takes life'. when my eyes opened, though the baby wasn't with me, but was fine. Alhamdulillah!

Lessons -

- Before giving up, Try your best first.

- Difficulties need patience and Trust to solve.

- Leave it to Allah, after trying your best

- Forr sure, Allah helps those who trust him.

- Do what your duty is, before blaming others.

- some problems only solution is patience.

- Giving up is never the solution.

HUMILIATING IS NOT ADVISING

I had a very old friend of mine, i considered her the best one but she after a certain time changed. she started to question me, my work, my habits and everything. Although she was the only one whom I trusted, but with time everything changed. Even when i was expecting, she taunted me of my upbringing and never left a moment to make me feel sad. At first I cried and felt embarrassed by her changed behaviour, secondly i tried to argue by putting up my point . but at last i realised that accepting her as a friend was my mistake because A friend never does what she did.

Lessons -

- Making others feel embarrassed is not funny at all.

- What you think is your opinion not a rule to be followed by everyone.

- Everyone has their own choice, solution and perspective to deal with their life.

- Just because, your idea works doesn't mean it works every time and with everyone.

- Respect others choices and accept them too

- Do not force others to follow you.

23

ADVISE WITHOUT INSULTING

When i was in the teaching field, I was an inviligator in the classroom. After the end of examination, a student ran towards me and informed me that a student was cheating and threw away the chit after exam, which she handed over to me. I called the student, who cheated and handed him his chit and asked about it, he accepted his mistake and i said , "i won't report it, let this matter be closed if you won't repeat it". He felt guilty and happy because i didn't insult him in class. All this was done when he was alone. I met him after a year, and he said that he hasn't shared the incident with anyone nor has he cheated again.

<u>Lessons -</u>

- Advising privately increases the value of Advise and the advisor.

- Insulting to advise is wrong.

- Before advising, think all about it's Consequences

- Correct others mistake privately

- Do not give the major punishment for a minor mistake.

BE JUST EVERYTIME

I was in the teaching field when it happened that a student disrespected the teacher, The real matter was the teacher shared an intimate joke which irked the student , and the matter reached the student's parents and manager of the school. I went to talk to that student, i tried hard to make her apologize but, she said "Mam! you know well about his behaviour yet you are standing quiet,". This made me realize that i was going wrong. I managed to bring the real matter to the notice of the principal and thus, the matter came to an end by warning the teacher and student.

<u>Lessons -</u>

- Not every time, younger ones are wrong.

- know the real matter before judging.

- Be just because Allah loves the one who is just.

- Try your best to handle the wrong people.

- solve the issue without disrespecting.

- Disrespecting is not always the solution.

- If you're the elder or at higher post , this doesn't prove you're always right.

- Justifying even after being wrong, is the loss of self respect.

PATIENCE HAS NO LIMIT

We often learn most things of life from our elders. As we grow, we start to understand the actual reason behind their activitives. one such of my relative is very patient and righteous one. she is above 85 of age but i never saw her reading with spectacles or even praying by sitting. she prays tahajjud, reads Quran and with no problem of sleep lackness which is becoming common even for youth today. she went through a lot in her life which shows her patience like living in a cottage for 15 years, losing her husband, son, daughter-in-law, brother, younger sister and even her house. yet nothing brought her faith down, she earns by stitching clothes even at this stage she often calls me her sister due to our similarity. I meet her regularly for she has something positive to share Always.

<u>Lessons -</u>

- when words fail, your patience speaks.

- For sure, Allah rewards you for patience.

- you lose nothing, if you have Allah beside you.

- Age is not a reason to lower your worship.

- your patience is greatest courage to fight.

- Indeed, you'll be loved if you love Allah first.

DO NOT ACT FOR ATTENTION

I was around 13, when i faced breathlessness due to excessive running. I felt extreme difficulty to breathe. My teachers later helped me to calm down by rubbing my palms and legs. My parents later picked me up from school for rest. I caught everybody's attention due to my condition that day and tried to falsely create this ruckus again by acting just to get attention from others twice in a month. My parents knew well that i was acting, so at the very moment, they corrected me by making aware that Allah knows the intention very well and i later corrected myself.

Lessons -

- Never act to gain other's attention.

- Indeed, Allah knows your intention.

- Do not take advantage of other's love.

- The more you act/lie the less will the people believe you.

- Do not be ungrateful

- Do not misuse your health.

- The biggest lie is the lie you say to yourself

KNOWLEDGE BEGINS AT HOME

Right from my childhood, i loved reading but with my parent's hardwork, it became a habit to read about the religion. My parents helped me to complete the Quran at the age of eight and allowed me to fast at 7 years. They always encouraged us towards the religion. my mother always narrated the stories of companions of prophet during our bedtime. when any of our siblings completed reading the Quran , she made sweets for all. She helped us to read islamic books ,and asked us often to pray nawafil, on weekend days, she dictated us stories and asked us to write them in english. My father would ask us to say what we learnt on religious classes, they always made sure to let us learn the religion in a fun way ,so that we learn and enjoy.

Lessons -

- Children learn from their home's atmosphere right from their birth.

- The more you're strict you are with your Religion, the more is the chances of higher reward.

- Let learning be your habit not a duty.

- Introduce religion to little one's in a fun way to let them learn it easily.

- Religion is easy but important to follow.

RESPECT YOUR TEACHER

I studied Quran , under a single teacher for more than 12 years, we were rarely given a leave. our teacher never spoke about other things and punished us rarely. yet, we had more fear and respect that we couldn't lie to him. once it happened that he beat me for not revising a certain portion of Quran and i cried hardly, but later my mother made me realise that this beating of yours will have a huge reward in paradise. for this pain was for your religion and this statement encouraged me to read more and more with understanding. my mother never allowed us to take a leave for these classes nor she accepted any disrespect towards our teacher.

Lessons -

- Never disrespect someone who makes you learn the religion.

- Let your suffering be an encouragement to learn more .

- The pain you endure is a proof of love for religion.

- Gaining knowledge is every muslim's responsibility.

- The best time to learn is from birth to the death.

DO NOT CAGE THE CREATURES

when i was around 10 years old, we had a small tenthouse to play. we got bored to play in it ,after few days we all decided to cage some pigeons in it and we took great care of them. but a few days later, one of the pigeon died. we were heartbroken upon seeing it , we held it in our hands and dig a grave for it. when my father came to knew about this, he made us understand that "you all as humans got bored in this tent house. then how can you expect birds to live in it which are actually meant to fly." so, atlast we all decided to release the rest of birds.

<u>Lessons -</u>

- let not your love stop others from growing.

- caging someone is not a way of loving.

- some things are meant to be the way they are, Do not alter their natural habits.

- Correct your mistake upon realising.

- your happiness is not real, if it is by hurting others.

RESPONSIBILITIES ARE BEAUTIFUL

My son was around 6 weeks old, when i left him at home and went out for my cousin's marriage for a while. everybody asked me about my son and one of our women's religious woman too asked me, I replied "he's at home. and now am going back for my duty (motherhood)". I gave the same reason to everyone but she responded me "not a duty but a beautiful responsibility," . she choose to correct me instead of laughing like others. This didn't made me embarassed , instead i was happy to realise that my son wasn't a duty, her words gave me energy and sadness for not enjoying my own family's marriage vanished.

Lessons-

- Sometimes Allah gives you a huge blessing without you asking for it.

- If Allah has blessed you with a great responsibility, be thankful.

- whatever is your responsibility, you'll be accountable for it.

- your own happiness is your primary responsibility.

- Do not take your blessings for granted.

- Be thankful for everything.

PRAY AND SUPPLICATE OFTEN

I still remember spending my childhood often being sad, for not celebrating birthdays. but today i feel so happy that My mother never bought a new dress infact, we prayed two rakat on this day and Supplicated for our bright future. My mother was very strict in the matter of prayer. We often prayed two extra rakah during our school tests or exam, she didn't fed us till we prayed. Today, those are the moments i cherish, how strict was she for religion which she instilled in our behaviour and daily life too.

Lessons -

- Pray and supplicate every now and then

- You'll realise the value of religion soon or later.

- Be strict in your religion's values & matters.

- your younger one's follow you, so be aware of your actions.

- Do not change your decision out of love.

- Remember, children take shape how you mould, so take care .

- Today it may seem their faith too difficult to follow, but one or the other day you'll feel unattractiveness towards sin.

SERVE THE GUEST BEST

I was raised in a house where every week, once or twice guests would come. we would welcome them warmly. often these guests were my father's friends who were religious and my dad often host those who come as a guest for islamic lecture. It was a routine for us to introduce ourself and convey salam. As I grew up, i saw my mother making good food and arranging it with enthusiasm. while serving my mother would say "this dish is less "and my father would understand that he should be moderate while eating. They didn't said but would understand each other. I saw this sign of understanding between a couple in my home thereby making me realise that a couple must understand each other.

Lessons -

- serve your guest first and give the best.

- serve in the best manner with respect.

- Do not backbite about your guests

- Guests are a means through which Allah . relieves stress or your difficulties.

- Talk, serve, and behave well while hosting

- Thank Allah for letting you host .

- consider the guests as a blessing but not problem.

FAITH HAS NO BOUNDARIES

I still remember, one of my teacher was leading the prayer and i was beside her. she Started to recite Surah Al Qiyamah and tears flowed through her eyes. we stood silent and i was amazed because we often hold back our tears but her faith knew no boundaries. she recited a verse thrice, i later went back home and read the surah with translation out of curiosity and i byhearted the whole surah. This was the impact her faith had on others.

Lessons -

- Don't let your faith (imaan) decrease because of situation.

- Let your faith have an impact on others.

- change your condition not faith.

- Do not comprimise with your religion in any manner.

- When you recite Quran, contemplate reflect, understand, follow and apply it in daily life.

- Be firm and clear in your faith.

- Have a heart which fears and eyes that allow fearful tears to flow upon the recitation of the Qur'an.

ALLAH GUIDES WHOM HE WANTS

Since childhood, i was an admirer of clothes, jewellery, heels etc . but as i grew up and understood islam, i realised that world is not a place to showcase my beauty and i started to wear hijab in marriages. No one asked or forced me, nor i felt uncomfortable when i started to wear it. Months later, my own sisters started to accept hijab and today, my cousins started to accept and follow. I never had any intention to force them nor i tried to convey the importance, it was Allah's plan. I also have been blessed with a spouse who encourages me to abide by my hijab strictly.

<u>Lessons -</u>

- Be firm on on your religion

- Do not force others to follow Islam

- It is Allah's will to guide.

- people follow what they see not what they hear

- Once, you decide just follow and trust Allah.

- your beauty is precious, don't lose it by showing off.

- Do not change your decision, if situation changes.

GIFT THE VALUABLE

Gift is the word, which makes the reciever and giver very happy. I was also excited to open the gifts of my marriage. There were Chocolates, steel vessels, photo Frames etc. Gifts were the same, which one could easily imagine if it was for the wedding. There wasn't happines in my heart for recieving but I was grateful and accepted it. But, one gift which was handed to me after a week of my marriage was from my Aunt, who wasn't financially stable. yet, she gifted me Quran (word to word translation), this gave me a feeling of calmness and peace, upon recieving and reading it. This is the only gift which am going to use till death in sha Allah.

Lessons -

- Gift, valuable and precious things.

- precious should not be the price but the smile of the gift receiver.

- Take care to gift which is usable.

- Try your best to make your gift a source of sawab-e-Jariya [deeds aftes death]

- The Best gift is QURAN.

LOVE OTHER CREATURES

We often by being superior creatures fail to value other creatures of Allah. when i was studying degree, i often saved money to have a chat at canteen and after eating, the crows always feed on remaining from the wrap of chat. This gave me an idea of spending 20/- rupees weekly and i started feeding the crows . I never loved Crows but i continued doing so till a year. I initially started to put some pieces and run away out of fear but now the crows fly near me closely as soon as they see black color(hijab). This journey was so loved and everybody were amazed at how crows flew over me as soon as they saw me. This not only increased my courage but also grew my love towards birds.

<u>Lessons -</u>

- Allah's other creatures deserves love.

- Love creature for the sake of Allah.

- let not the fear stop you from doing good.

- Do not do good deeds to show off.

HELP THE NEEDY

I was in class four, and during the month ramadan there was a committee who collected amount to serve clothes for the poor. My father Sent us to participate with them and we did so accordingly. It was around evening and there was very less time to break the fast. At the end, there was only a set of clothes remained, we knocked at the door but nobody came to recieve. so, we (kids) entered and saw a physically disabled man with only one functional hand, it was a dark room, we looked at him. We placed his clothes and ran out of fear but, today i still feel guilty of doing so.

<u>Lessons -</u>

- Feed as much as you can to poor.

- Help the needy often and regularly.

- Teach your kids to help the needy.

- Be grateful, when you see disabled ones.

- spend some time with people of special needs.

- Take your kids to meet people who are disabled or people with special needs.

LOVE THE UNKNOWN TOO

once i was going to college, when i saw an old lady walking and i offered her a lift .It became a routine for us atleast thrice a week to share our way. she used to share her story that she works in a hotel to earn for her daughter whose husband left her and she also had a major operation recently. Her story shook me that we act ungrateful to Allah even with so many blessings around, we complain about things we don't have, but at other side a women thrice of my age was working hard to feed her family. this woman and her story still gives me a lesson for whole life.

<u>Lessons -</u>

- Love others , even if you don't know them.

- Sometimes, unknown teaches valuable lessons for life.

- Being grateful, keeps you happy & content.

- Complaining makes one ungrateful.

- sit with unknown people, talk with them as people love to be heard.

- As Human ages, he desires only a ear to hear the words filled with love.

ACCEPT YOUR MISTAKES

We went to hydrebad to meet my elder sister who was reading (urdu, Arabic) there. After the meeting, when we were about to leave she said "father, i can't live here". As the wardon was very strict and she was the only elder student. she faced very difficulties during the week. my father tried his best to make her understand, but she didn't listened. Atlast, My dad cried saying "o my daughter, please forgive me for i couldn't teach you urdu/ Arabic during your childhood". It would be the painful moment for any of the child to see tears in our parent's eyes. After a long Conversation, she finally agreed to read and stay.

Lessons -

- some mistakes are meant to be corrected.

- Allah gives chance to correct your mistake.

- Mistakes haunt you in future, if you don't learn from it in the past.

- Learn to express your emotions to loved ones.

- Expressing your love makes bond stronger.

- Ask forgiveness, if you have wronged someone.

- Accepting mistakes is a sign of good human being.

LEARN TO SAY SORRY

My dad returned home, and asked about my sister and i said, "she hasn't reached from college yet". just then, my dad realised that he answered her call a while before and replied that he will come to pick her up. Before my dad could go to pick her up, she came back home with a frown face. She said that she came back by walking. My dad felt extremely guilty and he instantly replied "Maaf karo beta (forgive me, my daughter). He felt sorry for her.

Lessons -

- Your role doesn't defies the purpose of asking forgiveness.

- Mistakes happen by everyone, correct it by asking sorry.

- To forgive is minor deed while to forgive people is major.

- forgive even if they haven't asked you.

- Remembering other's mistakes will only make your heart heavy.

- know to let go other's mistake.

GOOD NEVER FOLLOWS BAD

I was on a trip with school students, we had a great start. Teacher made them to recite supplications, Aytal kursi. etc. A while later students recited some surah which i helped them to learn. After a couple of minutes they felt bored by being quiet, one among the student asked something to a teacher who nodded her response as yes. The student ran back to her friends and they began to sing Songs (film). I couldn't believe that the students knew those songs, and just before anyone could stop them. The bus just rammed onto a bridge stopping with a strong force, and we all were saved. we were shaken by the sudden break of the bus . The Principle stood in anger, and asked students to thank Allah for saving us and repent for singing songs.

<u>Lessons -</u>

- you cannot steal by saying BISMILLAH.

- Remember Allah everytime not only in need.

- Allah protects you as long as you remember him!

- Don't be arrogant, if you did a good deed.

- Supplication saves you from unimaginable dangers.

- you cannot guarantee your destination based on your deeds.

NEVER BE LATE FOR CHARITY

we had a senior leader [basheerunnisa sahiba] who always shared a joke during Eid-ul-adha which carried a message. she said that there was a man who sacrificed a goat on Eid. A few days later, he had a dream where, he saw numerous goats in jannah and found a goat with only 3 legs at a corner, He looked at it and realised it was his goat, and asked it, where is your other one leg to which it responded in your home's refrigerator. The Man woke up and saw the leg and later gave it for charity, This carried the message that one should give as much as he can before the time ends.

Lessons -

- Give only for sake of Allah.

- Do not be stingy when you spend.

- The More you spend for Allah's sake, more will be the reward in hereafter

- Remember whatever you have is from Allah

- Give the best first.

PERSONALITY NEVER DIES

I was newly married and was in initial trimester of pregnancy, that i came to know one of my elder teacher(Mohtarma Fahimunnisa sahiba) passed away. I couldn't believe, when i heard it, all through the night, i was having only her thoughts of how she introduced me to religion and helped me to lead the prayer for the first time in ramadan. early morning, i left my home for her funeral. It was around 80 km and all through the way i had nausea yet, my condition didn't stopped me. Although, i didn't met her for a year, but i wanted to see her for one last time and Alhamdulillah i reached on time. She was famous for her fearless nature and she learnt writing in her 40s and left this world inspiring everyone around her. May Allah bless her with the highest level of Jannah (Aameen)

Lessons -

- carry your personality in a way that inspires others.

- Help others with the talent Allah has blessed you with.

- Be the type of leaders, who leads others.

- Spread the knowledge till your last breath.

- There is no age to learn what, you Love

LOVE, FOR ALLAH

I joined quranic classes, on the first day there was a girl who was just looking at me.

but the following day she started smiling by looking at me, and moments later she came near and asked my name, and said "i really like you".

I had an exhausting schedule but that one line brought a smile and made me feel energetic and refreshing. This is what it is to like someone for the sake of Allah.

Lessons -

- Don't waste your time in hating someone

- say good and be good with everyone.

- your one smile can change many things

- Love for sake of Allah

- praise others if you want to

- It is not important to love only the known ones.

MEET,FOR ALLAH

The most amazing thing i've got from the social media is earlier someone joined my live session. she(Aysha) said that she lives in the same location. After a few days, she identified me in an islamic gathering among 100's of people without actually seeing me before . Till today she comes to our home to read Quran once a year in the month of ramadan. we often check out at each other. if Allah wants, you'll meet and you'll have to love each other only for his sake.

Lessons -

- Love each other for Allah's sake

- Some relations are made of love.

- Bond becomes special if it is for religion

- Try to contact your neighbour, friends for Allah's sake.

GIVE WHAT YOU HAVE

My 7/8 year old nephew(Afaan) was getting ready for prayer, when my uncle gave him 100 rupees note as gift. A while later, her mother gave him ten rupees and asked him to give it to poor people near the masjid. After he returned, he said to us he has nothing in his pocket as he gave all what he had which was 110 rupees. we were shocked upon hearing this but he left us amazed that even after knowing that it was quite large amount he gave it to poor because he wanted to give all what he had, and expressed it to us happily.

<u>Lessons</u>-

- Do not be sad after giving charity.

- whatever you spend will be returned on judgement day.

- Do not show off while giving the Charity.

- let your kids learn giving Charity.

- Let your hand and heart be always open for charity.

RUMOURS SPREAD FAST

I went for my exam by missing one of the family gathering early in the morning, after my exam there was huge crowd near my college as a burnt dead body was Found and thus investigation was carrying out. upon reaching home, i told my cousin about this, that i saw a dead body, where police was also present. A while later, i went to the family gathering and my sister asked "did you called the police after seeing the dead body?". i said "what!". she said "everybody is saying that.." as my cousin informed about this, i was so confused either to react shocked or to have laugh at this rumour. This is the speed of the rumour that it reaches before you.

Lessons -

- Rumours are carried faster than you think.

- Do not judge others based on rumours.

- clarify the rumours before passing the judgement.

- Do not pass the rumours & be a fool .

- 90% of the rumours are false.

- Do not be a rumour carrier.

PAST CANNOT BRING THE DEAD

I had a hectic day & was busy . At 7:30 pm when i got a call from a relative who was ill since a year wanted to spend some time with me. so i went forcibly as i was tired, upon reaching there when he got to know how busy i was he said "yeah yeah! you kids have become so big, how can you little kids manage time to meet ill ones". Upon hearing this, i got so angry that i left the place feeling that he's being ungrateful that atleast, i came all alone at night only to meet him & i left the place without informing him.few months later, i got the news that he wasn't with us, as he passed away. till the time he was buried, i was only expecting him to come back atleast for a while, so that i can ask him to forgive me for my behaviour but all that were just my perceptions because in reality he left us.

<u>Lessons</u>-

- Meet as if your meeting others the last time.

- Regrets /guilt can't bring the past back.

- what's over cannot come back

- Do not over react, where love was expected.

- How hard your life may seem, meet every relative specially the ill one.

ALLAH WILL SAVE YOU

I went with my grandma for her health checkup. when i parked my vehicle, a big stone fell at nearby place, i thanked Allah for saving me as i was at that spot Just before a while. Later, we stopped at a medical store, i was on my vehicle waiting for her, just then a bike passed through me who was hit by a fast moving bus, i Could have been the victim if the bike didn't passed by me. I was saved by Allah twice on same day and i realised it later , that i performed ablution before leaving and read the supplications which indeed saved me miraculously.

Lessons -

- Turn back sometimes in life only to see how Allah has saved you from disaster.

- Be thankful as you don't know , how many times were you saved from unseen disasters.

- perform ablution and remember Allah wherever you go.

- Read supplications often.

DON'T NEGLECT INTENTIONALLY

It was around 11:30 at night, that my dad asked us to come at a place to meet our head (organisation of woman) . i intentionally didn't performed ablution as i was late. i drove fast as the road was empty and dark, and i found my dad waving at me on other side of road, so, i took turn without even noticing the bus which was coming behind with full speed. And just by mini second i missed the bus & was safe. i realised things could have turned worst only by looking in my father's eyes filled with tears. I was thankful that Allah saved me from a disaster.

<u>Lesson -</u>

- No matter how busy you are, perform ablution / pray

- •Don't rush, because rush is dangerous often.

- If you're saved, first be thankful instead of like acting nothing happened.

- Thank / remember / repent to Allah often as he is the one who saves you in an unimaginable way.

TIME CHANGES

I was engaged & mostly expected that to be the happiest day of my life, but on the next day my father called me to a government hospital to help a girl. i earlier thought not to go but yet i went, after meeting the girl i got to know that a day before she was going for her aunt's funeral with her family but vehicle overturned and she lost her father. The only thing she said repeatedly to herself when her relatives came to pick her was "o my family, have patience don't cry". I witnessed how she was crying when she was alone in hospital and now she was the bravest to help and support her family. i had many questions that how a single day was very different to two people of same age .

<u>Lesson</u>

- Life may not be same for everyone so be kind.

- If you are happy you see someone is sad, do not express your happiness.

- sadness needs to be addressed first

- Do not ignore others by thinking that one will overcome their sadness by themselves.

- Help others when you see them in despair / difficulty.

INNOCENCE IS BEST

I was teaching at a course for kids below 10 years & we asked kids to bring vegetables, so that we can give them the knowledge regarding the nutrition each vegetable has. many of the students brought tomatoes as it was in everybody's home. As The class finished we asked every kid to take back their respective vegetable placed on the table, one among them stood near the table, staring at it for for a while, upon asking she replied, " i brought a tomato and now i don't know which one is mine" we laughed so hard at her innocence. That indeed the kids are the most innocent ones .

<u>Lesson:</u>

- Sometimes being innocent is important.

- Don't let the childish innocence in you die as you grow

- Innocence is a quality admired by everyone.

- everybody should have innocence.

ANSWER, ONLY IF YOU KNOW

I was in 4th standard, when i was fasting as we stood in school assembly , when one of my friend asked "we can't drink while fasting but our spit also has water, is our fast valid?" . we were confused, so we asked our class teacher who was a muslim, she was in hurry & thus she said "yes, it has water, so you can't swallow it" . Thus, me and my friends spent the whole day spitting until we were tired and our mouth was dried. i still remember how hard that fast was just because of someone's ignorance we had a hard day of fasting.

Lesson:

- If you have no knowledge regarding a matter then don't advise.

- Do not answer if you have no knowledge.

- Just to avoid someone stop answering incorrectly

- before you speak Advise only if you feel it is important.

- Do not feel insulted if you don't know about a subject.

SMILE, AS IT MATTERS

I was going to home depressed after my job due to an arguement with collegues, i had a choclate which i unwrapped but before i could eat , a seven years old student came towards me and wished me "good evening miss, bye miss". i couldn't reply so, i gave her choclate and just smiled back, A few days later, she came back with her friends in office room wishing me and said to her friends "this is the teacher, who gave me chocolate" . she turned towards me saying "i will not forget you teacher" . The only best thing happened on that day was the smile she gave, and I smiled in return with zero words exchange.

Lesson:

- smile because sadness isn't going to change the situation.

- Focus on one positive thing among 100 negative things.

- smiling though costs nothing but is precious .

- know the difference between smiling, laughing & humiliating.

- smile because it's sunnah and smiling is also a form of charity.

- smile because it's sunnah and smiling is also a form of charity.

TRUST ALLAH

I was only 15, but matured enough to wear a complete hijab, though at first i was forced to wear hijab & thus never accepted it with all my heart. After a year, when i was going to college with my friend (non-muslim) a guy followed us on a bike for long time, i noticed him but ignored. But a while later, it became serious , we changed the route but he came and stood right in front of us holding a bunch of Chocolates, he parked his bike and started to come towards us with flirty eyes, i couldn't even look upto him, i was all just thinking "what If someone sees me & informs my father /relative about this" though i don't know him yet i feared, it was the center of our city, among many people he dared to come near us, i was chivering & all of sudden we ran back from other route before he could follow us in college we were in the classroom. My friend rushed towards the washroom crying uncontrollably saying "my father would kill me, i am already living at my relatives house, he's following me since many days" - she turned towards me and said "you're lucky enough that nobody could see you as you're protected enough" her words shook me from inside & i realised how lucky I was, that i belong to islam & Alhamdulillah am a hijabi woman.

<u>Lessons -</u>

- even if you don't like it , just trust Allah.

- follow Allah's order and At the end, you'll realise Allah's plan

- The world will make you fall into the trap of nakedness, be brave to protect yourself.

- Have patience, for sure you'll be rewarded if you follow religion.

- If you follow this fake world, one or other day you'll fail

- Following the rules of religion may seem difficult but not impossible.

ONLY ALLAH CAN HELP YOU

I attended an engagement party where i had an ice-cream (Gola). The next day, my neck swelled. 3/4 days later i went to a doctor & he gave me some medicines which had some content making my body allergic in turn they created ulcers in my food pipe and when they reached my tongue i realised I couldn't even Swallow, i checked on doctor and he said "seems like you had allergy" thus advised me to have to injections but i hadn't enough dare so he asked me to go to a city. The city doctor looked and asked "how you lived with such severe pain" and he gave a liquid to gargle, it happened that the next day after gargling twice all my gums swelled. It seemed like my teeth would fall off right away. i couldn't drink nor eat i was drinking Juice with straw for three times a day, for about 20 days, i couldn't speak it was three constant jumah that i Couldn't read surah kahf loudly. yet i became arrogant thinking Allah gave me this he should solve this why should I ask him to relieve the pain, every night atleast three handful of blood was coming out through my mouth, yet i remained arrogant. Only after a month, when i was explaining something in action to express my mother my needs but she failed to understand me and that was the moment i broke & after a month, the first painful tear left my eyes describing my whole month journey & i finally cried before Allah for so long that from next day i started healing and after two weeks i started eating like a 6-month old baby eats solid food.

And this painful journey still makes me cry yet i realised some of the valuable lessons.

<u>Lessons-</u>

- Don't challenge your creator

- cry only before Allah because Allah understands your tears too

- you don't need a tongue, you need a heart & an eyes filled with repentance to cry before Allah.

- ·Trust Allah in every situation.

WHERE IS YOUR HAPPINESS

I met a man named Khalid, in workshop of Bangalore, he usually had conversation during the tea time in morning and once i joined them on my father's advice. Khalid sir initiated the Conversation by saying that he met a man. who said "i'm really happy, have luxurious Cars, bungalow-etc" so, he asked "where are those?" The man replied "i can't bring them here" , so khalid sir responded 'how can you be happy, when these arent with you here". The man stood stunned because those materialistic things brought him happiness and he would be sad if those were lost. khalid sir gave a beautiful answer that "happiness is what you carry everywhere. happiness lives within you safely which doesn't depend on anything or any person"

LESSONS -

- your happiness should not be dependent

- Happiness lies in your heart only by being contented

- By being happy you make yourself & others happy

- Happiness has no scale to measure except feelings.

- Let your happiness increase by sharing.

- You will fail miserably if you try to find happiness in the worldly materials.

HARSH JUDGEMENT IS WORST

I attended a workshop, where i saw a woman with hijab but a high camel hump I tried to talk but couldn't, in the break session, i heard her elder sister advising her about hadith, where prophet said camel hump as a warning sign of Qiyamah. And i thought not to intervene but still she had the hump till the day. The next day, i saw her face with some marks on it, so, i thought she might have Covered her face because of it. At the end of workshop. i saw her and her hijab was properly pinned without a hump, i looked at her and said she was really looking beautiful and she smiled back which started a good conversation between us.

<u>LESSONS -</u>

- know the matter in detail before judging.

- Do not be harsh about other's character.

- Advise in a way which sounds good.

- choose good words to advise.

- Do not advise repeatedly.

- Encourage and appreciate when someone does good act

- Have a comfortable conversation before advising people whom you don't know.

TEACH RELIGION FIRST

I met a woman in my workshop, she wasn't a Part of it. yet she came with her two kids. I initiated the conversation with her because there was no other person to interact with. she said she didn't give her children the wordly education instead she is making them learn arabic and was doing homeschooling. i thought it would be difficult for kids to live without competing in this world. A while later, All of us participants went out for a break and the task was to climb a mountain we were on a talk and all of a sudden i saw the woman with hijab with her kids all alone letting the kids climb the mountain, first i thought it was weird because that was not a place for the kids to climb and there was no safety but from the highest view all i could see was a fighter woman climbing behind her kids asking them to climb alone without holding her hand. I still don't know, who she is, because she never lifted up her hijab, but i still pray for her and her kids As what she thought of giving is something that this worldly education fails to give. Today as a mother i feel what amount of courage a woman needs to stand at the opposite of this cruel world to teach the kids humanity & religion.

LESSONS -

- Learn to teach your kids religion first

- A mother is the first teacher.

- Provide the righteous knowledge for your kids.

- Teach the best of religion for kids first.

- Let your kids live their life with religion as it's foundation.

EVERYONE HAS A PAST

I met a woman who was a lawyer by profession. she was always friendly and a bit childish joking often how she could have been a mother today with a child of my age & we would often laugh about it. I still remember the day she opened up about her tragic past life of being raised by her grandmother whom she loved so much.

But, a dispute of words led her to leave her grandmother alone for a while and upon returning back she was shattered to see her dead. she explained how the horrific past still haunts her and the satan influences her to die every minute and blames her for her grandmother's death. she was crying Inconsolably, and after the workshop of that day, i was confused about how to approach her because she was smiling till the day but i didn't knew what to say that would console her . As what she experienced I never thought of going through something like that. But eventually the way she let the words out calmed her heart and she was the one who came & hugged me by saying the same joke, I was in a state of shock that how strong was she and for how long was she holding it & I still call her often to check on her. I always pray for her that may she live hapy forever and in hereafter too.

LESSONS -

- If you see someone happy doesn't mean they really are.

- When you hear someone's sad past then learn from it

- Be thankful if you hear someone's suffering that God saved you from this suffering.

SMILE IS INFECTIOUS

The sessions of break during the workshop days were with everyone who were present at the resort. being an Indian, there is always an excitement when you See foreigners, i always used to sit and chat with one or other. I met an old man whom i helped and he said, to me "you are a very energetic girl" . His words made me happy because i love to pass on the positive vibes.

 I also met a woman to whom i always greeted but couldn't talk much with her, this continued till a day, when i was extremely sad and during that break i managed to wish her, and she said " i always see you as a very cheerful lady that makes my day." that woman who usually Smiles back whenever I wish and never utters a word other than that, but on that day what she said was making me feel like, all those positive vibes were calling me for more energy. however, i loved whatever those moments were spent with her.

LESSONS -

- Greet others with a smile.

- A smile costs nothing to share.

- However your day was , you deserve a smile of happiness for yourself.

CARRY YOUR CULTURE

One of the moments, i cherish is when i saw a group of foreigners wearing traditional saree, and helped them in letting it handle. they thanked me but the moment to admire was when one of them whom i helped wished me luck for the future as she was leaving the resort, i was sitting at a Corner applying henna she asked "how beautiful is this, you drew it very well" . I asked "you want to try?" she was extremely happy and i could clearly read her face with shiny eyes showing how much she enjoyed it. At last, she said. "i will forever cherish this moment and am going to remember your face for life because i love Indian tradition." whatever it is always carry your culture and share it.

<u>LESSONS -</u>

- Carry your culture wherever you are.

- Be proud of your culture and share it.

- Introduce your culture with love and respect.

- Do not force others to follow your culture.

- Respect others even if they don't follow your culture.

TREAT EQUALLY

There was a worker in the resort we stayed during workshop, we had an hour long break after lunch and she used to come to clean the pool everyday. I used to sit near the pool and watch the fishes running around and i loved talking with her, she and I used to have a minute chat daily. And on the last day of my workshop, i met her and said goodbye and hugged her to the extent that we had tears in our eyes . And at that moment, there came a man, who witnessed this was actually invited by my dad to the workshop and my action made him to attend that day till the end, my dad was very happy when the man said that to my father by pointing out to me but i was not aware of this. later, when we reached home, my father said "That hug of yours to a cleaner has cleaned heart of my friend"

<u>LESSONS -</u>

- Do not talk according to their profession.

- Let your emotion be true like your heart.

- Do not degrade others if you are blessed more.

- Do not be arrogant of yourself.

RESPECT EMOTIONS

There were a group of lecturers from AL-AMEEN college kolkata, who were attending the workshop as participants. I always asked those lecturers "why is this choclate so chocolaty" & we all shared a great laughter. on this, A few days later, i was trying to have a tamarind from tree & out of nowhere a lecturer helped me. while he was busy in phone I thanked him and shared the tamarind with everyone. on the last day of workshop, the lecturer called me on stage and said "this young girl, aged 20 is energetic, talkative, friendly and sweet just as the choclate she eats everyday, she reminds me of my sister whom i lost a year before and I Still miss her, but when i saw this girl, you always make me to remember her, i just pray that may this girl have a beautiful life ahead." I got very emotional that someone lost their loved ones and trying their best to be happy and am grateful that Allah made me a reason for people like them to smile.

<u>LESSONS -</u>

- Respect others emotions.

- Try to be the way you are.

- Carry a cheerful smile because you have it.

- Let your smile brighten your day and others as well.

LET YOUR PAIN OUT

on the fourth day of workshop , i still remember that i gathered all the strength i had to share my story, where i was struggling, to get over it. My father's brother was very ill, and he asked me to to come over for a talk, i was quite busy that day yet i went to have a look at him. when he came to know that i was appointed as a teacher, he said "yeah, yeah! why will you come to meet me when you are so busy in your life" & i got so angry by hearing & thinking that he was being ungrateful & i left the house without greeting. A month later; the news came that he was no more and my heart broked. I was filled with guilt that out of my arrogance, i didn't talked to him and i carried that guilt with me for over a year, until the day of workshop , i was crying so hard that my father hugged me and consoled me to the extent that he couldn't believe how much i was holding it inside. I am still thankful because i never hugged my father till that day and I felt that every single tear of my guilt was making me free by getting out.

LESSONS -

- The more you carry your guilt , the more it aches your heart.

- When you feel it's heavy, make your heart lighter by putting out

- If you can't express your pain, let your tears do so.

- Only your loved ones knows how to console you.

- Check on your loved ones often for the emotional support.

YOU NEED TO PRAY

My father and i were all prepared for the ten days workshop, my father after reaching out their didn't wanted to attend as he thought i would not feel open to share, but i made a deal that let's just live as participants and he agreed.

 for the Starting 4 days, i saw my father trying hard to understand the english language and the conversation . i saw him feeling sleepy and ignored. I still remember that it was the fourth day, i could not see him in that state any longer, l left my class, heading to my room, made ablution and prayed for half an hour, crying & praying to Allah that "o my lord, he stayed here because i requested him and he has paid from the amount he worked hard and i can't see it getting wasted, o Allah, my father loves to learn, please open all the doors of knowledge for him and allow him to learn in the easiest way" . I ended the prayer and Alhamdulillah, after the break, i noticed that every session had urdu and english language too. I couldn't believe that my supplication was accepted so soon. my father is my strength who loves to read and learn. I still think of that day, that how my heart craved to run towards my lord, to pray for my father.

<u>LESSONS -</u>

- Pray if your heart is constantly asking for it.

- Pray for your loved ones often.

- Pray , supplicate and never lose hope

- Sometimes, things change only when you supplicate.

- Miracles happen only when you try hard for it.

ENCOURAGE EVERYONE

At the end of everyday session of the workshop, every participant had to share what they learnt, and on the first day i wrote a poem and everyone loved it and encouraged me to the extent that today i wrote two books of my poems today.

I still think of the day as the most blessed one because whatever you learn is waste until you follow and it was pretty visible in the way everyone encouraged me by clapping and asked me to continue it.

A news reporter who was a participant Published my poem in the magazine and i felt extremely proud of myself, blessed by my lord, And grateful for this talent I am also thankful for my father who let me carry on my talent and everyone who encouraged me by listening to my poems.

LESSONS -

- Your Little encouragement can help others to achieve their aim.

- Do not degrade or defame other's talent.

- Appreciate others talent instead of being jealous.

- Learn to help others even if it saying a kind word or gesture.

- Try to showcase your talent without thinking about others.

GIFT OTHERS OFTEN

on the first day of my workshop every participant was provided with an identity card and a diary to write notes in . I didnt even opened the given diary, my co-participant asked me about this, i said "my elder sister loves writing in diaries, so I am keeping this as a gift for her," and i was writing my points in my other notebook. Till the end of the day, she called me and gave me another diary by saying "your diary is a gift for your sister, let this diary be a gift for you. from me" I thanked her for this kind gesture.

LESSONS -

- Gifting others make you happy.

- Try to gift others often.

- Be thankful for the person you received your gift from.

- it is not important to gift only the people you know.

- if you see someone is in need of something try to help them.

KNOW THE REALITY

when i was in hyderabad, with my mother for the workshop, we reached hotel and there we saw a guy with a very messy appearance, he was about to checkout from the same room we booked. so we stayed until he did so, the manager asked him about the advanced money but the guy replied that he paid it earlier. this conversation turned up into a heated arguement. me and my mother thought that the guy must be lying until the manager arrived and checked the footage and saw that the guy paid. The manager asked him to forgive & let him go. this taught us a lesson that the appearance has nothing to do with the character.

LESSONS -

- Do not make a perception without knowing the Reality.

- Character has nothing to do with the physical appearance.

- Not all perceptions are wrong, but recheck before terming it as reality.

- Reality is what actually is, and the perception is what you think that to be.

- Treat others according to the reality not according to your perception.

ACCEPT YOUR PARENTS

I attended a 3 day workshop with my mother in Hyderabad , i usually don't like travelling but those 3 days changed me in a way that led my mind open to face new challenges

Earlier, I used to get irritated by my mother and her presence was making me feel embarassed until i learnt about reality and perspective. i had a perspective about her and i thought to change it. Because my behaviour was Surely making her upset,

 i was feeling guilty for not having my father with me in my workshop, i was feeling angry because she couldn't speak english and was trying to talk to new people in urdu, I failed to notice she was learning, just like me.

I still feel bad for my behaviour but Alhamdulillah at last everything changed. i promised myself to accept my mother for how she is. And i am proud to have her, because since the day i was born she took great care of me and i know she'll always continue doing so.

LESSONS -

- Accept your parents as they are.

- Express your love towards your parents often.

- The most important form of love is to respect.

- Whenever your parents get hurt by your behaviour, ask forgiveness as soon as possible.

- Hurting your parents, doesn't guarantee you happiness in life too.

List of Contributors

The other books written by the author are-

GOLDEN ADVISE OF PARENTS

HALAL LOVE STORIES

UNSAID FEELINGS

MY JOURNEY OF DYS

ISLAMIC LULLABIES

ADVISE FOR THE WISE

WHAT LIFE TEACHES YOU

You can follow the author on social media as-

Nabi_e_ummah on Instagram
Or
Charge_ur_eemaan on Instagram
Or
www.firdosetarannum@gmail.com

Notes

In the name of Allah with Whose name nothing can harm on earth or in heaven, and He is the All-Hearing, All-Knowing

O Allah, You are my Lord, there is no god but You, in You I put my trust, and You are Lord of the mighty Throne. Whatever Allah wills happens, and whatever Allah does not will does not happen. There is no power and no strength except with Allah, the Most High, the Most Great. I know that Allah has power to do all things and that Allah has encompassed all things by His knowledge. O Allah, I seek refuge with You from the evil of my own self, and the evil of every creature that You hold by its forelock. Verily my Lord is on a straight path

O Allaah, Lord of Jibreel (Gabriel), Michael and Israfeel, Creator of the heavens and the earth, Knower of the unseen and the seen, You are the Knower of the unseen and the seen, You will judge between Your slaves concerning that wherein they differ. Guide me to the truth of that wherein they differed by Your leave, for You guide whomsoever You will to the Straight Path

O Allah, help me, guide me, correct me, enable me to attain what is right and earn reward, and forgive me if I make a mistake or am deprived of an answer.

O my Lord! Open for me my chest (grant me self-confidence, contentment, and boldness); And ease my task for me; And make loose the knot (the defect) from my tongue, (i.e. remove the incorrectness from my speech), That they understand my speech

-Aameen